Don't Eat the Teacher!

Nick Ward

For Nats, Tully, Fin . . .
and all their teachers!

Scholastic Children's Books,
Commonwealth House, 1-19 New Oxford Street,
London WC1A 1NU, UK
a division of Scholastic Ltd

London ~ New York ~ Toronto ~ Sydney ~ Auckland
Mexico City ~ New Delhi ~ Hong Kong

First published by Scholastic Ltd, 1998
This edition published by Scholastic Ltd, 2000

Text and illustrations copyright © Nick Ward, 1998

ISBN: 0 590 54321 0 (Hardback) 0 590 11325 9 (Clubs and Fairs edition)
0 439 99626 0 (Paperback)

Printed and bound in China

All rights reserved

2 4 6 8 10 9 7 5 3

The right of Nick Ward to be identified as the
author and illustrator of this work has been asserted by him
in accordance with the Copyright, Designs and Patents Act, 1988.

"Hurry up, Sammy!" his mother called.
"You'll be late."
Sammy dived downstairs for his breakfast.
It was his first day at school, and he was
very, very excited!

But when Sammy became too excited,
he had the unfortunate habit (as all
young sharks do) of biting things.

Sammy opened
his mouth and . . .

"Oh, Sammy," complained his mother. "Don't eat the table." "Sorry Mum," blushed Sammy. He grabbed his school bag, kissed his mother and swam out of the door.

"Be a good boy, Sammy," cried his mother. Sammy and his dad drove down the lane to Sammy's new school.

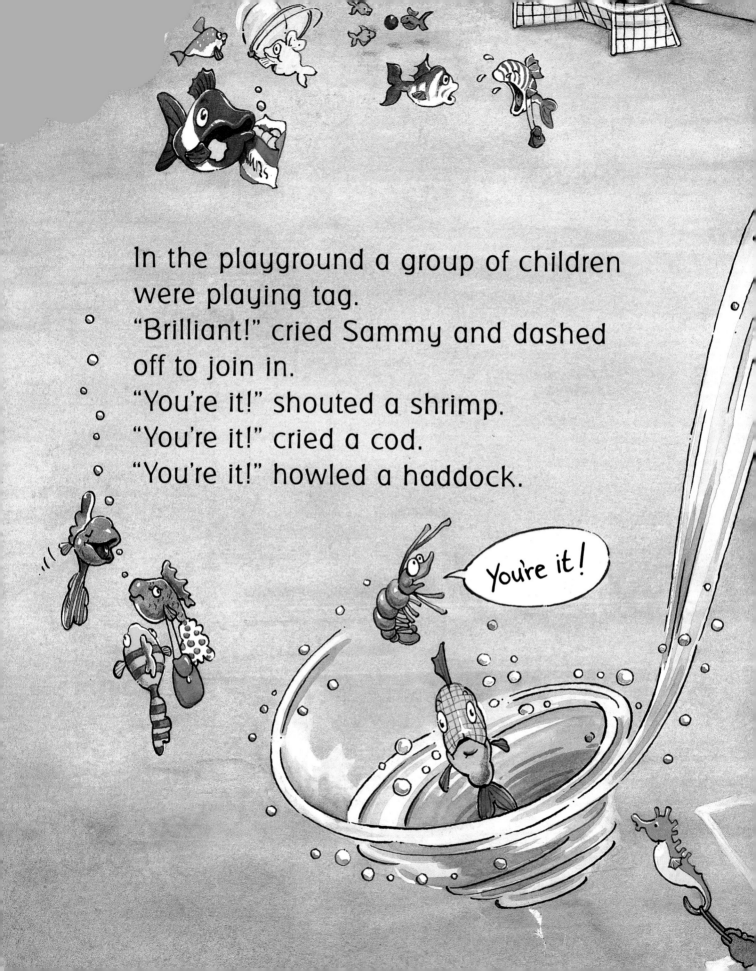

In the playground a group of children
were playing tag.
"Brilliant!" cried Sammy and dashed
off to join in.
"You're it!" shouted a shrimp.
"You're it!" cried a cod.
"You're it!" howled a haddock.

You're it!

Sammy opened his mouth and . . .

"Oh, Sammy," the children moaned.
"Don't eat your school friends."
"Sorry," blushed Sammy. He hiccuped
politely and out swam a little fish.

The bell rang and all the fish swam off
to their classroom.

"Good morning, children," beamed
the teacher. "Let's start the day with
a really good story."
"Brilliant," thought Sammy, flapping
his tail in excitement.
"Here we are," said the teacher.
"Here's a story we can really get
our teeth into."

OUR OBJECTS
TABLE
Interesting things
we have found.

Sammy opened his mouth and . . .

"Oh Sammy," cried the children.
"Don't eat our story!"
"Sorry," blushed Sammy.
"Never mind," smiled the teacher.
"Let's try some painting instead."

Splish! Splosh! Sammy loved painting. He was so excited, it was hard not to nibble his paintbrush. "Finished," he called.

"Sammy, that's lovely," said the teacher. "It looks good enough to eat." Sammy opened his mouth and . . .

"Oh Sammy," groaned the teacher.
"Sorry," blushed Sammy.
"Never mind," said the teacher, giving
him a cuddle. "It's music now."
"Music and movement," called the teacher.
"As I play the piano, I want you all to
pretend you are seaweed, swaying
in a gentle current."

"I'm seaweed," thought Sammy, drifting and stretching as elegantly as he could.

"The current is getting stronger," sang the teacher. The children started to dance even faster. Sammy started to get excited.

"Now you are a storm," the teacher cried. "A terrible storm destroying everything in its path."

"I'm a terrible storm!" Sammy yelled. He opened his mouth and . . .

"Oh dear," thought Sammy as he got ready to go home. "I didn't mean to. Tomorrow I'll be good . . . really, really good!"

"Hello, Darling," said Sammy's mother
at the school gate.
"How was your first day at school?"
"Er . . . brilliant," said Sammy.
"And what did you learn today?"

"Lots," blushed Sammy.
"Don't eat the stories,
Don't eat the paintings,
Don't eat the classroom and . . ."

"Don't eat
the teacher!"